Me.

A Poetry Book By: Cyanne Hackney

For every big dreamer who can't seem to just pick one.

Author's Note

When I started this book I was 13 years old. My Thoughts were scrambled, my grammar was bad but I was proud. I was proud because I did it. I created something that grew with me, everything that changed me as a person, every flaw, quirk and weird thing about me I was able to put into words and express. So yes, it will be hard to read sometimes and you might not understand but that's okay. It's okay because I understand. I hope you enjoy Thank You for reading. - Cyanne

Love Fall, Hate Summer

I love the Fall

Fall is Taylor and Lana
Pumpkin Spice and Pink out days

Screaming August on the first and looking back on how October passed you by in the rain

you're not alone in the Fall but you are alone in Summer

In Summer you don't go to parties or play sports you stay home because it's so hot you could faint

I hate Summer. It's the first day of school but Summer is not over. You can still barely breathe outside.

It's the first day of Fall and it's suddenly Friday Night Lights and Homecoming the haunted house and halloween reading books and baking cookies.

I love Fall, I hate Summer

Fake

I am real and fake
I wonder what would happen if I could read minds
I hear the rumors spread
I see the whispers and stares
I want to dissolve into the wall
I am real and fake
I pretend to not let it bother me that it's all good
I feel the tears coming
I touch them with shame
I worry I might not get through this
I cry in silence
I am real and fake
I understand two wrongs don't make a right
I say the stretched truth
I dream of being liked
I try to fit where I don't belong
I hope for real friends
I am real and fake

Grown

Growing up means

Realizing that

Only you know

What you want

Not always what you need

Pink

In Kindergarten I loved pink, pink and princess and rainbows and glitter, pink was happy, pink was home, In third grade I wanted to wear blue and skirts sucked pants where everything because the popular girls were not to girly they were cool and I wanted to be cool too,fourth grade and I still hate pink and that's okay except now boys dont like you, they don't like girls who are tough and smart so in fifth grade I started wearing pink again the color I needed to hate and I failed on purpose because I thought I all I needed was a boy not an A, in sixth grade I thought I was gay. I still wore pink because I started to like it but no skirts because girly girls are straight,in

7th grade I abandoned pink because I was Non-Binary and it was to feminine, I wasn't straight but, I was a cheerleader who wore a skirt but not a girl I was Amari because I hated how my name sounded butchered and feminine like it wasnt legal and right pink sickened me so I wore black, white, green and gray, I'm in 8th grade now I don't regret my past I love my name but it sounds like a curse in my classmates mouths I wear pink and I love it my closets a rainbow but pink takes it over I'm a nice purple not just a pink or a blue I feel alone in the world I am not safe in but I feel safe in pink I am red, orange, yellow, green, purple and blue and all the colors in between. I am Pink

Alone

I always feel alone
I am hated and loved
I am forever alone

Too.

Too girly. Too rude. Too much of a prude. Too loud. Too quirky to be wanted in the room. Too white to be black but, Too black for my own good. Too MUCH. Yet I'm never enough, never heard, never understood. Too extra, to many toos.

Crush

I'm not anybody's crush. Sometimes I feel I don't deserve love. I am not the pretty girl people moon about to their friends most of the time I believe I'm not pretty at all because I don't look like all the other black girls with a silk press or braids and I don't look right with my little puff of hair, when I have crushes all they do is crush me, exhausted from trying I look in a shattered mirror so its myself I do not see for though its all I will ever be I am weird and flawed and I don't belong but maybe I thought if one person cares that's all I need I thought of people I would love from the moon and back and then I thought of the ones who wouldn't love me. A crush is a dream and a burden but all mine were only the last. Is it bad to want to be wanted to be the one pursued to be a crush and not crushed but that's a dream though it's not new because I'm nobody's crush.

Friends

I have friends in a way by force maybe or the obligation to be with the lonely girl because it makes you feel like a good person but at the end of the day most are fake. The rumors spread the group chats made its all jokes though when they know I know, I'm hated enough to have no one but known enough to always have someone I'm the last picked for sports and the tantrums thrown by my teammates make me second guess my love for the game but to study for tests wanna be my partner you can do all the work I don't know how to. I walk through the halls alone and eat by myself at lunch. I am kind to others not the other way around because kindness happens behind the scenes too. I don't have friends but I have friends.

Thoughts

Thoughts are valuable, fragile so

Handle them with care for

One day you might change

Unkind, unnurtured, damaged

Groggy

Hearts, heads and souls

Thoughts

Save

Mirror

I hate my reflection but I like pictures of me but only the ones I take because other people do me dirty and then I look ugly. when I post I use gray filter and low exposure because you can't see me in the dark I hate my hair because I never know what it's going to do I feel like I need to be glued to a mirror or I'll get weird looks from others whom already think im ugly then some days the mirror is my best friend and I wish it was the camera because then I would look lovely in pictures of me then I start to see bumps and bruises and scars and I fall apart cause I am not pretty I only look that way I'm flawed and not in a good way I want to see the crumbs on my face or how my smile looks or when the color drained from my lips I hate mirrors but they are the best sometimes they even give me hope.

Shut up

I can't shut up.
I raise my hand in class and it's ok it's time to give somebody else a chance and they laugh.

I start talking and I get excited so they roll their eyes and now I'm holding my tears back cause I don't wanna cry

The next day I go on about me too much to say when everyone wants to flee

So I stop because I've now scared them away. Maybe they will listen another day.

I can go on and on about books. Do you want to know where I read them, my secret nooks?

But no they dont they just stop and stare, throwing me weird looks because who even reads let alone likes books?

So I shut up again my face unbothered but my heart still hurts so I go drink some water my face burning getting hotter and hotter but this poems going nowhere so it's time to stop all this jaunter

About stories no one's listening to but souls above so I'm signing off now cause I know they have to run even though no one stopped me and all my fun.

Why do I scare you

Why do I scare you? Is it the brown hue I can't control are you scared of melanin is it the big words I know what I want to inquire is why do I scare you is it my curves or my stature is it the way my hips move is it the fact that I have opinions although most teen girls do is it that i refuse to do your bidding aligned with being a slave to you is it my intellect that you believe threatens you I don't believe you understand but I am not here to scare you in fact I am not here for you to pour you a glass of reality in fact I am here to recognize a tragedy I was fortunate not to see with my own eyes for not to be that crime but people treated that simple knowledge as a prize like freedom or rights because people like you were scared what a knowledgeable black girl can do but if I scare you I should because even if you're scared at the end of the day I'm still good.

State of Mind

I am not faking for attention. I just don't know what to do. I panic when I'm surrounded by people crowded in a room. I lose track of time and the day because I am still trapped in the maze of yesterday about what happened in.. who did what... in 1607... god life is tough my state of mind is broken what even is a memory my mind recites the words unspoken but doesn't keep them safe for me I don't remember I say as the days fade away I hate the remembering game just keep my thoughts far far away my state of mind is broken will it ever be repaired are all my words unspoken lost in there the state of my mind crumbles my pulse feels as though my heart is in my head about to explode all these voices in my head screaming wanting to be heard I try to fight them for peace while I think go to sleep and they'll be silent although now its my dreams they intrude I scream enough is enough but now I sound crazy because who am I talking to I am now silent laying painfully awake thinking how did I break.

Whitewashed

What is black?
Why am I *too black* for people and *too white* for others?

but the thing is I'm not white not at all apparent by my skin but I guess because of how I move and dress I seem to much of it

because I speak *white* but what does that mean is it to washed to speak clear and complete well you sound *white* what do you mean the voice I was born with the one I use to lead the one I can't control the one god gifted me

Well, you dress like a *white* girl well then explain how white girls dress I'm just trying to be comfortable no need to be pressed and since when did clothes have a race just be glad I am dressed because I am still a teenage girl who doesn't rest and deals with utmost stress

You say I'm whitewashed but maybe that's good because I am not *ghetto* and I don't want to be associated with the hood or with people who treat me as though I'm misunderstood.

Young

You are

Only just being your

Unique story don't

Neglect you before you're

Guaranteed to succccd

Love Hard

Some might say I love hard. I doodle until my hands go numb pictures of us full of hearts and love I am lungs and everyone is nicotine killing me slowly sucking up all of me and I'm giving and giving and pushing it out because I don't know any better I care for people who don't care about me hoping that one day they will see the girl who wants to care about them ever so badly my friends say I'm too nice but I already know I try to act tough but my gaps won't close so I make playlists write poems and doodle some more until my hand are bleeding blistered and bare so i recite this now over and over till perfection is a given till i have given all I can give until I have loved too hard.

Rose with Thorns

Let them be roses i'll be thorns always the apple of their peers eyes whilst I get clipped off, thrown away, set to the side

Thorns hurt people, make them bleed so you clip them again, file them away because people don't need pain

I'd rather be a rose though easy and carefree maybe I wouldn't be hated or here whispers about me

But being a thorn is cool too, though I may not fit in, popularity can't make me happy right? A better person because I'm liked?

I want to be a rose with thorns sharp but safe liked and loved not tossed away

Free to be, to lead or to follow. I'd rather be a rose that wilters not one that's not artificial or fake, one that makes mistakes and sometimes needs a break

The one that makes other people happy, that's beautiful and strong but let them be roses. I can be one too. I'd rather have thorns though.

Edge of 14

I'm hanging on by a thread edging myself closer and closer until i'm one inch from falling off a cliff made of negative thoughts, anxiety and depression the whispers and rumors about me the voices in my head saying they want my life to be over they want time to stop the ones that doubt I can make it to 14 all my intrusive negative thoughts.

To Be.

To be known.
To be heard.
To be healed
To be forever
To be loved.
Loved.
To be loved by the famous
To be known.
To be loved by the mute
To be heard.
To be loved by the mender
To be healed.
To be loved by a writer
To be forever.
To exist forever
Be known forever
As ink on a page or
Words on a screen.
To be.

Dear --friend

Dear Future --friend, My name is Cyanne like the color though not spelled the same C Y A N N E that is my name. I love books and clothes, music and food but you probably already know that, you're my --friend but I'm still talking to you. I really hope you're nice and that you haven't lost enough pride to still treat me like a princess from time to time. I'm an overthinker, that shows in how I text. always second guessing your responses to my statements left. Know I'm not a burden and you have no need to feel trapped. I can be a lot, Sometimes it's ok to take a step back. I wrote this at 14 on a warm day in June lying on my bed hoping for something more. I wonder how long it's been and why I'm sending it to you. My brain is a jumbled mess from book ideas to stress most of the time just thinking about how I dress. I hope you feel the same way about me as I do you, that feeling whatever we choose. Thank you for listening to my ted talk type rant. I know it was intense. but goodbye cause I don't really know how to end this.

America is a teenage girl

America is a teenage girl slowly destroying herself from within, building up oceans of emotion in 50 different shades all special in their own ways. She says she wants to stay away from the drama but then always ends up in the middle of the war, always second to Britain because she's older, stronger and more mature. America is a cry for help never at peace with anyone nor herself. Her walls that she built are crumbling down even when she tries to hold it together by clowning around America is a teenage girl like me, different pages of a book for the whole world to see.

Before

I want to go back to before, before the looks and weird stares before we cared how we dressed, how we wore our hair.

When naps were punishment and not a reward when halloween was only about having fun not dressing like a whore.

When we wanted to live and not just survive when our main goal in life was just to not die.

When people believed in us when we could be whatever we wanted to be before when motherhood was still a beautiful thing and was not something we feared a victory to defeat

When makeup came shaped as pink hearts and butterflies when our lives were not centered around one day becoming wives.

Before when we ate candy till we puked not the now when we actually want to.

The before when I did not want to be you. Before version two.

Before my emotions were all purple and blue with a tiny orange hue when anxiety was joy and before fear turned to envy and the tiny red man became all tall and bleu

Before I was a teenage girl and before I knew.

Silent

I wasn't always silent. I was the one who would never shut up. I was always the annoying one no one cared for. I would joyfully ramble about my greatest feats but that never made sense to anyone but me. Silent is what I became when I found enough. Enough laughter, enough wary glares, enough hatred to shut up and be silent enough to stop living, enough to start surviving, enough is never enough until those are the last words on your breath, silence. silent.

Girl

Pick me girl. Mean girl. Shy girl. Sweet girl. Girly girl. Girl's girl. I am just a girl. But wait, that's not -- it cannot possibly be true, that's not the only thing people see when I walk by that simply can't be right. Some people see an object, a toy to play with when they get bored, a target for their latest and greatest, a prize to be won because as a girl we are only good to look at, to touch , to cook and clean to reproduce but not to produce because that's a boy's job. Procreate but not create because why are you thinking anyway. Girls whom are supposed to be fragile and chipper eventually turn into women strong and bitter. Without wo there is man, men who were boys tarnished and deprived of real love in their lives because real men don't need love real men aren't pussies real men are strong real men aren't weak. And they are definitely not twinks. Boys do not act like girls, girls cannot act like boys they have to just be in a box until they can become a homemaker and a wife until they are barely living life. But this all okay cause boys will be boys and I'm just a girl right.

C-Y-A-N-N-E

Hello my name is -- when I call your name please stand say here, hi, present. Amer. here, Jody. howdy, Marlo. hi, Owen. hello, Makayla. present, Marcus. here, Kendlei. howdy, Mia. hi, Mason. hello, Amy. present, C-oh. Well, I'm not even going to try this one. Cyanne. What? I'm here. My name is Cyanne. Beautiful name sorry. Jacob. here, Gabrielle. Howdy, Jadrian? Cyanne fades because Cyanne doesn't get credit Cyanne gets oh, lord what is this Cyanne gets kyan ryan diane shyan Cyanne gets nothing of value Cyanne gets in nowhere of importance Cyanne is too much compared to Adrienne, Wayne, Aubrey, Caleb and Olivia too. Cyanne cannot be celebrated without being questioned first. Cy, Cece, ana all me but only a sliver, a grain a minuscule piece of the identity that is slowly cascading off my back Cyanne is me and I am she please do not interrupt me for I am going to say again Hello my name is Cyanne, Cyanne Hackney pronounced (Sy-Ann Hack-Knee) spelled C-Y-A-N-N-E thank you for your time.

About the Author

Hello! My Name is Cyanne Hackney. I am 14 years old and I live in Texas as a Freshman in highschool. Fun fact about me is I have tried every creative career I could think of and just decided that I was going to do them all. No, this is not my one and done. I have plans for a series, two stand alones and another poetry book in the future. For now though I'm just going to do me. Try to be myself and hopefully grow a lot. Again Thank you for read - Cyanne

Milton Keynes UK
Ingram Content Group UK Ltd.
UKHW020111050824
446426UK00013B/305